A Dozen Ducklings Lost and Found

Harriet Ziefert

Paintings by Donald Dreifuss

HOUGHTON MIFFLIN COMPANY, BOSTON 2003
Walter Lorraine ⌘ Books

*To the Pediatric Oncology Dept.
at Dartmouth Hitchcock Medical Center
for pulling our duckling out of a hole
—D.D.*

Walter Lorraine (wr) Books

Text copyright © 2003 by Harriet Ziefert
Illustrations copyright © 2003 by Donald Dreifuss
All rights reserved. For information about permission
to reproduce selections from this book, write to
Permissions, Houghton Mifflin Company,
215 Park Avenue South, New York, New York 10003.

www.houghtonmifflinbooks.com

Library of Congress Cataloging-in-Publication Data
Ziefert, Harriet.
A dozen ducklings lost and found : a counting story / by Harriet
Ziefert ; illustrated by Donald Dreifuss.
p. cm.
Summary: Between the pond and the farm house some of
Mother Duck's new babies get lost.
ISBN 0-618-14175-8
[1. Ducks—Fiction. 2. Animals—Infancy—Fiction. 3.
Counting—Fiction.] I. Dreifuss, Donald., ill. II. Title.
PZ7.Z487 Dp 2003
[E]—dc21
2002009403

Printed in China for Harriet Ziefert, Inc.
1 3 5 7 9 10 8 6 4 2

Farmer Donald had a pasture with twelve
broken fence posts, which he needed to take
out of the ground.

He used a shovel and a pickax and
his two strong arms.

He worked hard for a whole morning and
dug up the old fence posts, one by one.

Mother Duck had a nest with twelve white eggs, which she needed to keep warm.

She sat on her eggs for three whole weeks
until they hatched, one by one.

When the ducklings were ten days old,
Mother Duck wanted to show them off.
"One, Two, Three, Four, Five, Six, Seven,

Eight, Nine, Ten, Eleven...Twelve!
Follow me," she said as she marched them
in the direction of Farmer Donald's house.

Mother Duck walked ahead of her
ducklings, never looking back.

She was sure they were in a straight line
right behind her tail.

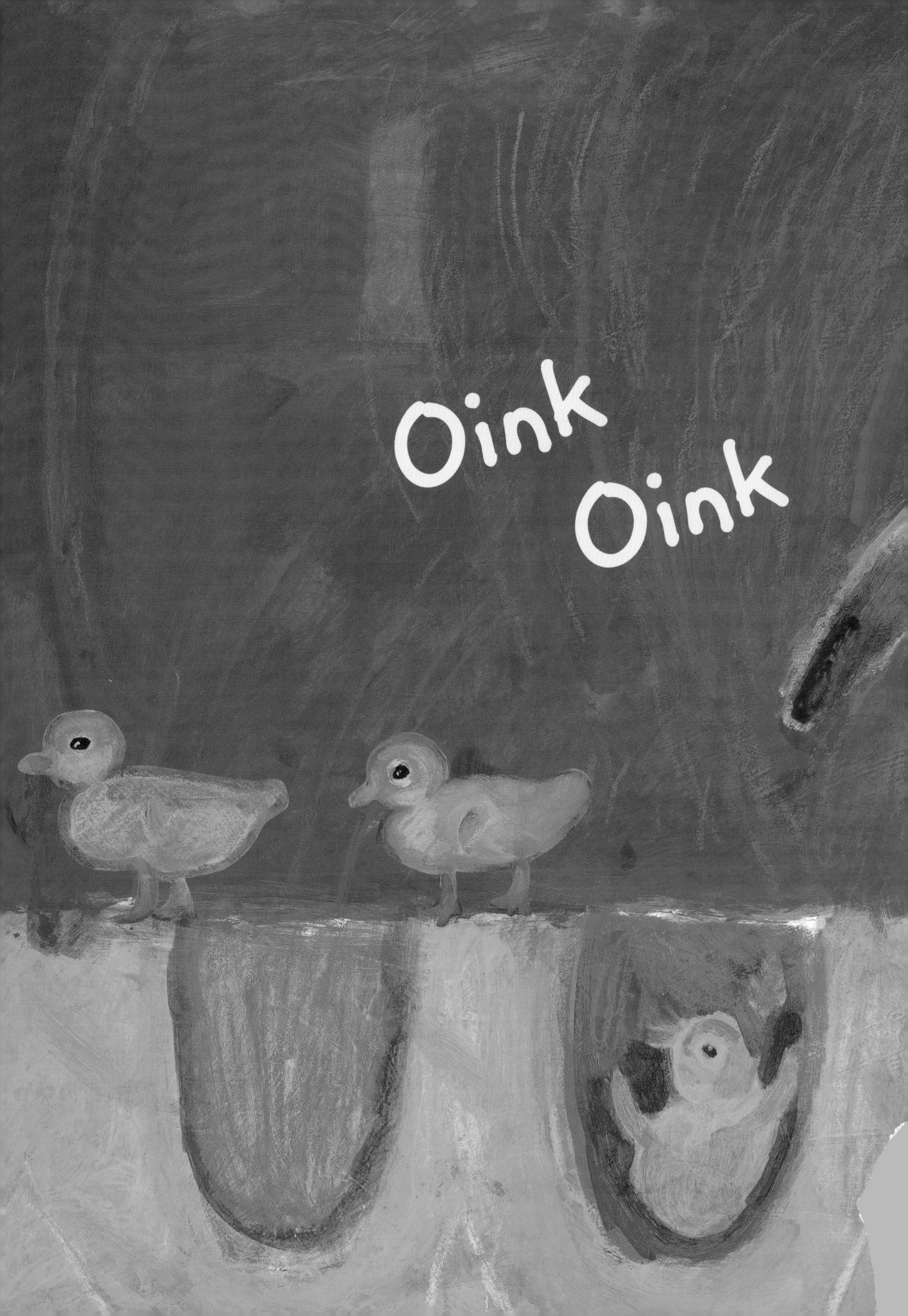

Oink
Oink

When Mother Duck finally stopped to count
heads, she saw only four of her babies.
She counted up:
"One, Two, Three . . . Four."

And she counted down:
  "Four, Three, Two...One."
"What happened to my eight other
ducklings?" she asked.

Mother Duck called:
　　"Five, Six, Seven, Eight, Nine,
　　Ten, Eleven . . . Twelve!"
But none of her ducklings came back.
She called again:
　　"Twelve, Eleven, Ten, Nine,
　　Eight, Seven, Six . . . Five!"

Farmer Donald heard Mother Duck's calls. "What's wrong?" he asked.

Mother Duck explained, "I had twelve ducklings—an even dozen—when I started. But now I count only four. I called my ducklings forward and backward, but I didn't hear peeps from any of them."

"Show me the way you walked from the
pond to the pasture," said Farmer Donald.

Mother Duck led the way. Then came her
ducklings. Farmer Donald followed with his dog.

The little ducklings heard rustling in the grass. They wanted to climb up and see what was going on. They tried and tried.

But they could not free themselves. They
were stuck, really stuck, and so they cried:
Peep!   Peep!   Peep!   Peep!

"I hear your ducklings!" said Farmer
Donald. "They fell into the holes where my
fence posts used to be."

Peep! Peep! Peep! Peep!

Mother Duck was happy—Farmer Donald
had carefully lifted all of her stuck
ducklings from the holes. Her whole
brood was safe.

Then she cried:
"One, Two, Three, Four, Five, Six,
Seven, Eight, Nine, Ten, Eleven, Twelve—
follow me!"

And they did—all the way to the pond.
Quack, quack, quackity, quack!

When Mother Duck turned around, there were twelve little ducklings—an even dozen— swimming all around her.

Farmer Donald says:

The farmyard ducks in this story are Muscovey ducks. They're descended from wild ducks, which came from Venezuela.

Laying eggs:
Ducks lay their eggs in the spring. They are white and about twice as big as hens' eggs.

Sitting on the nest:
After a duck builds a nest, she lays her first egg. Every day she lays another egg until the nest is full. A duck will usually start to sit on her nest after she's laid 8 to 12 eggs. It takes 34 days for them to hatch.

Inside the eggs:
A duckling starts off as a tiny dot inside an egg.
It feeds on the yolk as it grows. By hatching time, its
body almost fills the egg. Like a chick, a duckling pecks
its way out of the shell.

Newborn ducklings:
A newly hatched duckling doesn't need to eat or drink
right away—it just stays in the nest and is kept warm
by its mother. After two
days, the mother takes
all her ducklings to
find grass and water.

Growing up:
At first, ducklings are
covered in furry yellow down. They begin to grow white
feathers when they're a month old; some of the feathers
have spots. Some grown Muscovey ducks have white,
black, and brown
feathers.

After one year,
they're ready to lay
eggs and have
babies of their
own. Muscovey
ducks live for
about ten years.

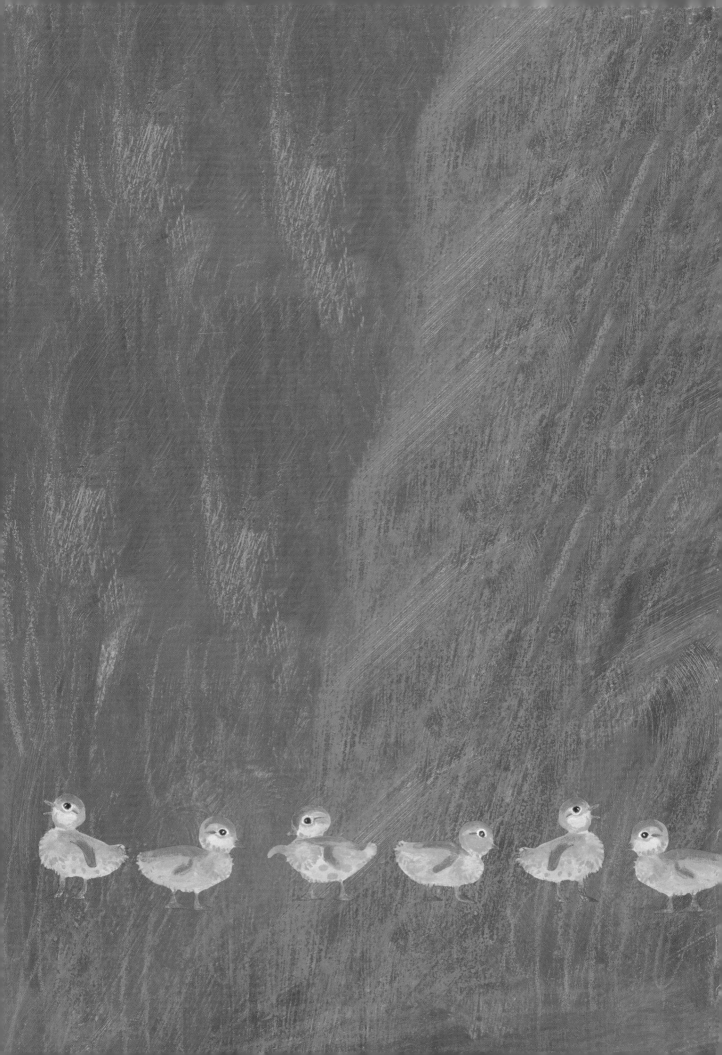